# The MONSTER Who Ate My PEAS

To my parents,
for giving me the love of language
—D. S.

For my son, Gabe
—M. F.

Published by
PEACHTREE PUBLISHERS, LTD.
1700 Chattahoochee Avenue
Atlanta, Georgia 30318-2112

www.peachtree-online.com

Manufactured in Singapore

Design by Loraine M. Balcsik
Composition by Melanie M. McMahon

10 9 8 7 6 5 4 3 2

ISBN 1-56145-216-5

Library of Congress Cataloging-in-Publication Data

Schnitzlein, Danny.
      The monster who ate my peas / written by Danny Schnitzlein ; illustrated by Matt Faulkner.-- 1st ed.
         p. cm.
      Summary: A young boy agrees to give a disgusting monster first his soccer ball, then his bike in return for eating the boy's peas, but when the monster asks for his puppy, the boy makes a surprising discovery.
      ISBN 1-56145-216-5
      [1. Peas--Fiction. 2. Food habits--Fiction. 3. Monsters--Fiction. 4. Stories in rhyme.] I. Faulkner, Matt, ill. II. Title.

PZ8.3.S2972 Mo 2001
[E]--dc21                                   2001021167

# The MONSTER Who Ate My PEAS

DANNY SCHNITZLEIN

Illustrated by

MATT FAULKNER

PEACHTREE
ATLANTA

"Eat your peas," said my mom, "or you won't
  get dessert."
I said, "Before peas, I would rather eat *dirt!*"
"I know you don't *want* to," she said with a glare,
"But until they get eaten, you'll stay in your chair."

I begged and I whined. I got down on my knees.
"*Please,* Mommy! *Don't* make me eat all these peas!"
I stomped and I grumbled. I yelled and I pled.
"Why can't I eat corn or potatoes instead?"

"Eat up those peas. Do it *now,*" my mom said,
"Or you'll get no ice cream…and you'll go straight to bed."

My mom left the kitchen. I poked at those peas.
Their sickening smell made me weak in the knees.
Quickly I offered the peas to my pup,
But Ralph barely sniffed them, then turned his nose up.

I closed my eyes tightly and whispered a wish.
*"Please* let these peas disappear from my dish!"
And something quite strange and mysterious occurred,
Almost as if somebody…somewhere…had heard.

For right out of nowhere a monster appeared.

His hair looked like spinach and so did his beard.

His big bloated body was broccoli-green,

And his breath, when he sneered, reeked of rotten sardines.

Each eyeball resembled a big brussels sprout.

His long bumpy squash-nose was sticking straight out.

Large liver-like lips peeled back to reveal

Sharp teeth like a shark's and a tongue
     like an eel.

Long octopus tentacles writhed from his torso.

Quite gruesome already, those arms made him
     more so.

His ears were like mushrooms,
     his chin like a beet,

And he balanced himself
     on two big stinky feet.

Just how he got in, I hadn't a clue.

My heart skipped a beat as I asked,
     "Who are *you?*"

He growled, "I'm the monster who helps kids like you.
I eat up their eggplant. I eat turnips, too.
I gobble down foods that make small stomachs quiver,
Like lima beans, collard greens, spinach, and liver.

I came in reply to your pitiful plea,
And I'm ready and willing to eat every pea.
I'll eat up the big ones. I'll eat up the small.
But then you must give me…
    your new *soccer ball*."

I thought of my soccer ball,
under my bed.
(I once bounced it twenty-three
times on my head.)
But then when I looked
at the peas on my plate,
My brain filled with dread
and disgust
and with hate.

"What is your *answer?*" the monster demanded.
"I don't have much time, so I'll be very candid.
Millions of kids want their yucky foods eaten,
From Bali to Raleigh,
from Chile to Sweden."

"Okay," I said finally.
"I'll give you my ball.
Eat up my peas.
Eat them up, one and all!"

He laughed a cold laugh
   as he picked up each pea,
And swallowed them down
   in-di-vi-du-al-ly.

All sixty-four peas—slimy,
   gruesome, and green—
He ate every one,
   and he licked
   the plate clean.
And after he'd
   licked, and
   he'd lapped,
   and he'd
   slurped,
He set down my plate,
   and he boorishly
   burped.

Then just as my mother came back in the room,
He vanished, no trace, with a noise that went *F-O-O-O-O-M!*

Mom looked at my plate and she shouted with glee,
"You did it! You ate each and ev-er-y pea!"
She gave me a hug and my ice cream, so yummy
With chocolate on top, so good in my tummy.

Then I went on upstairs and peeked under my bed.
I started to sweat; my heart filled with dread.
For there in the spot where my ball used to be

There was only

One very small

Squishy

Green

Pea.

And now when I want to play soccer with Dad,
I think of that ball…and I get very sad.
If I've said it one time, then I've said it ten,
I *won't* make a trade with a *monster* again!

Not long after that, we had peas with our meal.
The monster appeared with the same kind of deal.
"I'll eat up your peas, just as quick as you like,
But then, in return, you must give me…
    your *bike!*"

I thought of my bicycle, shiny and new.
I'd spent my whole savings to buy it. (That's true.)
        But when I looked down at those
            gloppy green peas,
        I felt like you feel
            when you get a disease.

"Okay," I said sadly, "I'll give you my bike.
Just eat up these peas. Get them out of my sight."

The monster then opened his mouth very wide.
He took all my peas and he dumped them inside.
He chewed and he chomped and he swallowed 'em down.
Then *F-O-O-O-O-M!* He was gone, off for some other town.

My mom served me cake, but I just couldn't eat it.

I walked to the door, feeling down and defeated.

I twisted the knob and I shuffled outside

To get on my bike and go out for a ride.

I looked all around and I started to cry.

My bike wasn't out there. (I think you know why....)

And right in the space where my bike used to be,

There was only

One very small

Mushy

Green

Pea.

Now when my friends take their bikes for a ride,
They never ask me, so I stay home inside.
If I've said it one time, then I've said it ten,
I *won't* make a trade with a *monster* again!

A week after that, there were peas in the stew!
The monster showed up, like he always would do.
The words that he said made my whole body freeze.
"Give me your *puppy*…
    and I'll eat your peas!"

I looked down at Ralph; he gazed up at me.
I looked at my plate, at each ghastly green pea.

"COME ON!" growled the monster,
  "I'M ALREADY LATE!
JUST GIVE ME YOUR DOG…
  AND I'LL FINISH YOUR PLATE!"

I looked at those peas and I just about gagged.
I looked back at Ralph; his scruffy tail wagged.
My pup put his cold little nose on my knee.
I reached for my fork and I speared a small pea.
I opened my mouth and I squinched up my eyes.
The pea touched my tongue…and I got a surprise.

That pea didn't taste like I thought that it would.
I had to admit it. That pea tasted—*good!*
I picked up another…and chewed it…and swallowed.
Each pea tasted better than those it had followed!

I ate every pea, 'til there wasn't a trace.
And Ralph thanked me kindly…by licking my face.

I turned to the monster, that grumpy old guy,
To say "I don't need you," and tell him good-bye.
But right in the spot where the monster had stood

Was

Only

A

Pea…

And it tasted quite good!

And now there's not one
    single food I won't try.
If others can eat it…
    well then, so can I!
I'm happier now
    than I ever have been,
And I *never* will trade
    with a monster again!